· TINY TALES ·

OF THINGS WE DO
AT CHRISTMAS

This book belongs to

....

....

Text and compilation Copyright © 1994 Michelle Lovric
Illustrations Copyright © 1994 Royle Publications Ltd

This edition published by Longmeadow Press
201 High Ridge Road, Stamford, Connecticut 06904, United States of America.
To order: (800) 322-2000 Dept. 708

Design and Color Reproduction by Camway Autographics.
Set in Utopia

Library of Congress Cataloging-in-Publication Number
ISBN 0 - 681 - 00761 - 3

Printed and bound in Singapore

First Longmeadow Press Edition
0 9 8 7 6 5 4 3 2 1

Produced by Royle Publications Ltd, Royle House, Wenlock Road, London N1 7ST, England.
Created by Michelle Lovric, 53 Shelton Street, Covent Garden, London WC2H 9HE, England.

·TINY TALES·

OF THINGS WE DO
AT CHRISTMAS

illustrated by Gillian Roberts
story by Michelle Lovric

LONGMEADOW
PRESS

 Christmas,

we hang holly on the door.

*W*e say "Merry Christmas"

to everyone we meet.

e

bring

smiles

to the

snowmen.

$\mathcal{W}$e hang pretty

ornaments on the tree.

 *C*hristmas
cards
come
every
day,

*A*nd
sometimes
presents
from
far away.

We go Christmas shopping,

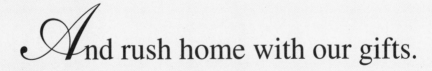
*A*nd rush home with our gifts.

$\mathcal{W}$e put everyone's Christmas presents

under the tree.

*S*anta always comes to our

Christmas party

And we kiss

under the

mistletoe.

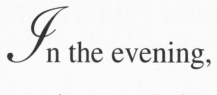

*I*n the evening,

we sing carols in the snow,

$\mathcal{A}$nd at night,

we read Christmas stories,

17

$\mathcal{A}$nd cuddle up in front of the fire.

On Christmas Eve, we try to stay awake
to wait for Santa.

19

$\mathcal{B}$ut Santa comes in the night
while we are sleeping.

*I*n the morning
our stockings are full!

We try <u>not</u> to wake up the grown-ups

too early on Christmas morning.

We love Christmas!

The End.

24